Let's Get A Pet

by Harriet Ziefert

illustrated by Renée Williams

HOUGHTON MIFFLIN COMPANY   BOSTON

Atlanta   Dallas   Geneva, Illinois   Palo Alto   Princeton   Toronto

"Look at all the pets!" said Mike.
"What will we get?"

Collie
Dog

3

"Dogs are good pets," said Mom.
"Let's get a dog."

"I know *dog*," said Abby.

"D, O, G is *dog*."

"Cats are fun," said Dad.
"Let's get a cat."

"I know *cat*," said Abby.
"C, A, T is *cat*."

"Look at the frogs," said Mike.

"Let's get a frog."

"I know *frog*," said Abby.

"F, R, O, G is *frog*."

"Look," said Abby.
"P, I, G—*pig!*
Let's get a pig."

"A pig?" said Dad.

"Pigs are not good pets."

"A pig?" said Mom.
"Pigs are not fun."

"A pig?" said Mike.
"Let's not get a pig."

"That pig is a good pet," said Abby,
"and that pig is fun!"

"What will we get?"
said Mom.
"A dog? A cat?
A frog? A pig?"

"Let's get the pig," said Mike.
"Let's take two!"

And that is what they did!